Dear Parents and Educators,

Welcome to Penguin Young Readers! As know that each child develops at his o. speech, critical thinking, and, of course, reading. Penguin Young Readers recognizes this fact. As a result, each Penguin Young Readers book is assigned a traditional easy-to-read level (1–4) as well as a Guided Reading Level (A–P). Both of these systems will help you choose the right book for your child. Please refer to the back of each book for specific leveling information. Penguin Young Readers features esteemed authors and illustrators, stories about favorite characters, fascinating nonfiction, and more!

MW01008444

Small Potatoes: Ride the Potato Train

LEVEL **2**

GUIDED READING LEVEL **E**

This book is perfect for a **Progressing Reader** who:
- can figure out unknown words by using picture and context clues;
- can recognize beginning, middle, and ending sounds;
- can make and confirm predictions about what will happen in the text; and
- can distinguish between fiction and nonfiction.

Here are some **activities** you can do during and after reading this book:
- Sight Words: Sight words are frequently used words that readers must know just by looking at them. They are known instantly, on sight. Knowing these words helps children develop into efficient readers. As you read the story, have the child point out the sight words below.

all	good	on	there
and	like	soon	they
are	look	take	up
down	make	the	well

- Rhyming Words: On a separate sheet of paper, make a list of all the rhyming words in this story. For example, *fair* rhymes with *there*, so write those two words next to each other.

Remember, sharing the love of reading with a child is the best gift you can give!

—Bonnie Bader, EdM
Penguin Young Readers program

*Penguin Young Readers are leveled by independent reviewers applying the standards developed by Irene Fountas and Gay Su Pinnell in *Matching Books to Readers: Using Leveled Books in Guided Reading*, Heinemann, 1999.

Penguin Young Readers
Published by the Penguin Group
Penguin Group (USA) Inc., 375 Hudson Street, New York, New York 10014, USA
Penguin Group (Canada), 90 Eglinton Avenue East, Suite 700, Toronto, Ontario M4P 2Y3, Canada
(a division of Pearson Penguin Canada Inc.)
Penguin Books Ltd, 80 Strand, London WC2R 0RL, England
Penguin Ireland, 25 St Stephen's Green, Dublin 2, Ireland (a division of Penguin Books Ltd)
Penguin Group (Australia), 707 Collins Street, Melbourne, Victoria 3008, Australia
(a division of Pearson Australia Group Pty Ltd)
Penguin Books India Pvt Ltd, 11 Community Centre, Panchsheel Park, New Delhi—110 017, India
Penguin Group (NZ), 67 Apollo Drive, Rosedale, Auckland 0632, New Zealand
(a division of Pearson New Zealand Ltd)
Penguin Books (South Africa), Rosebank Office Park, 181 Jan Smuts Avenue,
Parktown North 2193, South Africa
Penguin China, B7 Jiaming Center, 27 East Third Ring Road North,
Chaoyang District, Beijing 100020, China

Penguin Books Ltd, Registered Offices: 80 Strand, London WC2R 0RL, England

Copyright © 2013 by Little Airplane Productions, Inc. "SMALL POTATOES" CHARACTERS
AND LOGOS © and ™ 2013 LITTLE AIRPLANE PRODUCTIONS, INC. All rights reserved.
Published by Penguin Young Readers, an imprint of Penguin Group (USA) Inc.,
345 Hudson Street, New York, New York 10014. Manufactured in China.

ISBN 978-0-448-46365-0   10 9 8 7 6 5 4 3 2 1

ALWAYS LEARNING   PEARSON

Small Potatoes

Ride the Potato Train

by Josh Selig
illustrated by Cassandra Gibbons

Penguin Young Readers
An Imprint of Penguin Group (USA) Inc.

4

Look!

It's the Potato Train!

The Potato Train goes to the fair.

Hurry up and take us there.

Ruby drives.

Click! Clack!

Ruby drives down the track.

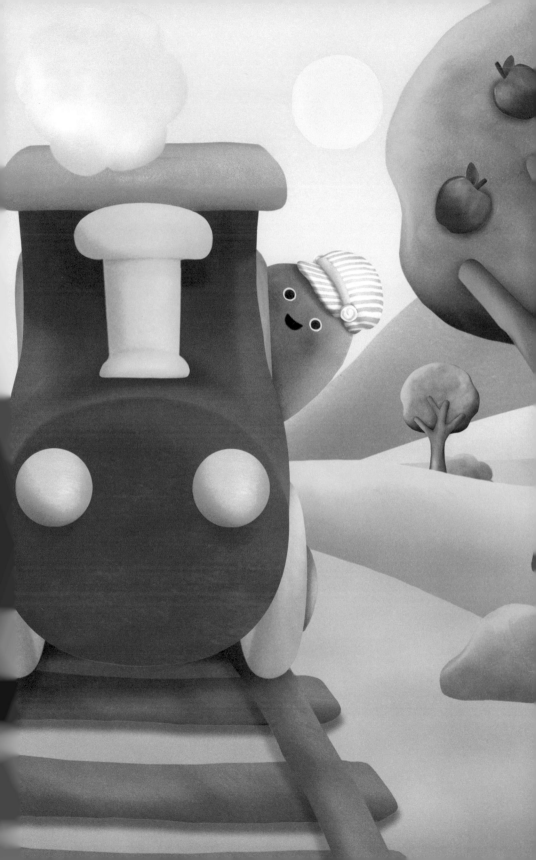

Chip loves the Potato Fair!

There are games to play

and treats to share.

Nate says, "Stop the train!

There is a sheep right in the lane!"

Olaf says, "Well, that's just great.
This sheep is going to make
us late!"

"Excuse me,
sheep upon our track.
Won't you please take
two steps back?"

The sheep is kind.

The sheep is good.

He steps back

just like he should.

The potatoes all start moving on,
and soon enough the sheep
is gone.

The train goes quick.

The train goes fast.

They pull up to the fair at last.

The Potato Train is at the fair.

The Small Potatoes

love it there.